Close to the Wind

David Orme

Published in 2002 by:
Nelson Thornes Ltd
Delta Place
27 Bath Road
CHELTENHAM
GL53 7TH
United Kingdom

02 03 04 05 06 / 10 9 8 7 6 5 4 3 2 1

A catalogue record for this book is available from the British Library

ISBN 0-7487-6417-8

Illustrations by Beverly Curl
Cover illustration by Rob Hefferan (represented by Advocate)
Page make-up by Peter Nickol

Printed and bound in Great Britain by T. J. International

Contents

Chapter 1

Perfect for windsurfing

The sun sparkled on the lake as the wind made small waves. It was a perfect day for windsurfing!

Twenty brightly coloured sails moved across the lake. The steady wind was moving them at a good speed.

Jackie Fuller had been windsurfing for two years. During the winter she had met up with a group of windsurfing friends. They had decided to form a windsurfing club. Now the good weather had come, the club members practised most days.

Jackie steered by pushing the rig – the sail, mast and boom – from side to side. She was also "feeling" the wind in the sail. To go fast you need to get the wind at just the right angle to the sail. People who have never sailed think that the wind just blows you along. It isn't as simple as that! Good, fast sailing means "reaching", sailing at an angle to the wind.

Jackie wanted to practise going fast before Saturday. The club had organised a race – down the lake, round the island, then back again. There was a small prize for the winner. Jackie didn't care about that. She wanted to show everyone how good she was. Especially the boys in the club. One or two of them were too big-headed!

"Tiny" Pembury was leading the sailing. He turned into the wind. All the other windsurfers turned too. When you are in a group, it is easier if everyone moves in the same direction. It stops people bumping into each other.

Jackie thought sailing into the wind was fun. Of course, you can't head straight into the wind – you have to go at an angle. Sometimes it's difficult to get this right.

Some of the sails started to flap. This is bad sailing. Jackie was pleased that her sail wasn't doing this.

Just then Jackie heard a noise coming from the end of the lake. She knew what it was. She groaned. Not again!

Chapter 2

Ban the motor boats!

The problem was that many different people used the lake. They didn't always get on with each other. Some people wanted to sail or windsurf. Others wanted to fish. All of these groups got cross with people in motor boats. Sometimes these boats pulled waterskiers and had to go very fast. This could be dangerous for other people on the lake.

The sailors and the fishing club complained to the local council. They wanted a speed limit on the lake. Even better, they wanted motor boats banned altogether.

The problem was the person who owned the boatyard on the lake. Mr Henshaw was an important local person. He hired out the motor boats. If they were banned, he would be out of business. Many of the people on the local council were friends with Mr Henshaw, so nothing changed.

People who drive motor boats can be stupid

sometimes. They think that because they don't actually hit anything, it's OK. They never think about what happens to the water behind them!

Jackie heard the motor boat getting nearer and nearer. There was no way that the windsurfers could get out of the way. The boat roared past, much too close.

The sailboards started jumping up and

down. Jackie just managed to stay upright, but other people fell off into the water. This wasn't serious — they could climb back onto their boards again. But the practice session was ruined.

Back in the clubhouse the club leaders had a meeting.

"It's the people who are staying at Pine Cottage," said Phil. "They've rented the cottage for the summer. I expect they've hired the boat for the summer too."

Everyone groaned. This could wreck the whole summer!

"I'll go and see them later," said Tiny. "They might be reasonable."

Chapter 3

Not reasonable

But they weren't!

Next day, Tiny reported back to the others. Tiny had got his nickname because he was tall and broad, but this hadn't impressed the people at Pine Cottage!

"Some flash bloke out to impress his girlfriend. Said it was a free country, and he could do what he liked. I asked him if he could stay off the lake just for Saturday afternoon so he didn't muck up the race. But he shut the door in my face."

Phil, Jackie and Tiny went to see Bob

Thomas. Bob was on the council, but he wasn't a friend of Mr Henshaw!

"There is some good news," said Bob. "You know that the government is thinking of making the area a National Park next year? That will make it much easier to ban motor boats."

"But what about this year?" Jackie asked.

"Sorry, I don't think there's much I can do."

The club had another practice in the afternoon. The flashy man wasn't out on the lake, which was good news. Most of the other motor boats went slowly. Sensible people wanted to enjoy the view, not rush up and down as fast as possible!

The practice turned into a friendly race. The wind was stronger. This was just how they liked it! The boards bounced over the waves, and it was almost like being at sea.

Sailing into the wind is great. You have to sail as "close to the wind" as possible. This means sailing as near as you can towards the direction the wind is coming from. A large fin called a daggerboard sticks down into the water. This stops the board drifting sideways. You can pull it up when you are sailing downwind.

Jackie came fourth in the practice race. Not bad – but she still had a lot to do if she was going to beat the boys!

Chapter 4

Flash Harry

The next day was hopeless. The wind had dropped, and it was cloudy and dull. It felt quite chilly on the lake and everyone wore wetsuits.

The man from Pine Cottage had decided to spend the day roaring up and down the lake. Tiny called him "Flash Harry" and the name stuck. He must have been annoyed by what Tiny had said. He deliberately came close to the windsurfers. They were worried that someone might get hurt so they gave up the practice for the day.

Some of the club members went home. The rest sat about in the clubhouse, working on their equipment and listening to music. They all felt very fed up.

Phil was in a bad mood.

"The race is going to be ruined. There's no point in going ahead with it," he said angrily.

Tiny sighed. "I don't see what we can do about it."

"Well, I'm going to do something," Phil replied.

Tiny and Jackie looked at each other. This sounded like trouble. Phil was a great guy and a good friend, but sometimes he did stupid things.

"What are you planning, Phil?" asked Jackie. "For goodness sake don't get into trouble!"

But Phil wouldn't listen. He didn't like being told what to do – or what not to do!

"You'll see," was all he said. Then he left.

Everyone else groaned. As if they didn't have enough trouble!

Chapter 5

A night visit

The lights of Pine Cottage were brightly lit. Inside, Flash Harry was playing loud music. It was a good thing that there weren't any other cottages nearby!

The cottage was surrounded by pine trees. There was a lawn in front of the cottage, going down to the water's edge, and a boathouse. This was where the motor boat was kept.

A dark figure was cycling down the road with no lights. Phil didn't need lights. He knew the road well.

Quietly, he stood the bike by the fence and

crept in through the gate. His old black tracksuit was just the job for creeping around in the
dark.

"I don't really need to creep," he thought.
"With that row going on, they'll never hear a
thing."

He slipped through the trees until he got to
the boathouse. The door was locked, but this
wasn't a problem. The front, facing the lake,
didn't have doors. Phil carefully scrambled
round the boathouse and slipped inside.

There was an old rowing boat inside, but
Phil ignored that. He jumped down inside the
motor boat. He stopped to listen, but the music
was still playing. Great!

Five minutes later Phil was on his way out of
the boathouse. Suddenly, he heard voices
outside the cottage!

Flash Harry and his friend had come out
onto the lawn. Phil could see two red glows –
they were smoking.

Phil realised that his black tracksuit could be seen against the white walls of the boathouse. He threw himself down on the ground, face down in the grass. The ground was cold and hard. He hoped they weren't chain smokers!

At last their voices faded, and he heard a door shut. He got up and ran silently out of the garden. His bike was where he had left it.

A good night's work! He couldn't wait to see what happened the next day!

Chapter 6

Stuck!

The next day was Friday. The windsurfers hoped to get a good day's practice in. A chilly wind was blowing across the lake. These were ideal conditions. As they went up and down the lake they would be sailing across the wind, or "reaching" both ways.

The weather forecast had said "sunshine and showers". Nobody minded rain, but they all wore their wetsuits. The lake water could be very chilly if you fell in!

They were soon moving down the lake. The wind came in gusts, and seemed to change direction from time to time. The windsurfers needed to work hard all the time to get a good speed.

Then came the sound they all feared. The roar of a motorboat came booming up the lake. As usual, Flash Harry seemed to be heading straight for them!

Then something odd happened. The engine of the motor boat started to splutter. Then it died. The surfboarders sailed past on both sides. Flash Harry was furiously trying to start the engine.

"Got a problem, mate?" Phil asked as he sailed past. He got a rude reply. As Jackie sailed past she heard Flash Harry's girlfriend moaning at him, telling him she was cold. Jackie was not sympathetic.

Then it started to rain. There was no cover in the motor boat. Unless Flash Harry could get it moving, he and his girlfriend were going to get very wet!

The windsurfers went down the lake, swung round the island and headed back. It was raining hard now. And the motor boat was still there.

A soaked and not very flash Harry waved to them.

"Can you help? We're stuck."

"That's not what you said last time," said Phil. "Why don't you ring on your mobile?"

SPEED250

"I can't get any reception."

Phil knew that anyway! "Looks like you'll have to row, then."

"Can't. The oars are missing."

"Oh dear!" said Phil. "You shouldn't come out without your oars, you know."

Luckily for Phil there was three metres of water between him and the motor boat.

Just then they heard the sound of another

boat. Someone must have spotted the stranded motor boat. Mr Henshaw was on his way! A great pity, they all thought. Still, the trouble-makers were soaked through by now. And it looked as if Flash Harry was going to have to find himself a new girlfriend.

Chapter 7

The race

Phil kept quiet about his night-time adventure. When Tiny heard that the motor boat had water in the petrol tank he guessed what Phil had done, but didn't say anything. Phil was smart. The engine would need to be stripped down. Flash Harry wouldn't get it back until next week!

By mid afternoon the race was in full swing. Bob Thomas had fired the shot to start the race. Now he was waiting in his boat at the finishing line to judge the winner.

Jackie was in a good position as they got

near the island. Tiny and Jake were in front of her. It was unusual for Jake to be in such a good position. Usually he came in about half way down the field.

The turn was a danger point. If the field was bunched up, people might run into each other.

Jake made a bad turn. Jackie sailed past him. Only Tiny to beat – but that wouldn't easy. Jackie had one advantage: she was lighter. There was less weight for the wind to push!

She crept closer and closer. She could see the finish with Bob Thomas standing up in his boat. Nearer, nearer – and across the line! But who had won?

Bob pointed to Jackie. "Jackie – by a nose!"

Jackie was thrilled, and everyone else was pleased too.

As they were celebrating, Phil pointed out into the lake.

An old rowing boat was heading for the small harbour. Flash Harry was having a hard

time of it. He wasn't used to rowing! His ex-girlfriend was holding a big suitcase and moaning!

"Great!" said Tiny. "Looks like they're giving up on their holiday."

Phil scratched his chin.

"Wouldn't it be funny if someone had pulled out the plug in the bottom of that rowing boat. They'd get really wet again!"

There was silence.

"You didn't," said Jackie. "Did you?"

"No," said Phil. "Of course I didn't. But I wish I'd thought of it!"

Sports ZONE

If you like this book, you may also enjoy others from the same series.